Monsters Not Allowed!

Tracey Hammett & Jan McCafferty

First published in 2010 by Scholastic Children's Books
Euston House, 24 Eversholt Street
London NW1 1DB
a division of Scholastic Ltd
www.scholastic.com
London ~ New York ~ Toronto ~ Sydney ~ Auckland
Mexico City ~ New Delhi ~ Hong Kong

Text copyright © 2010 Tracey Hammett
Illustrations copyright © 2010 Jan McCafferty

HB ISBN 978 1407 11017 2
PB ISBN 978 1407 11018 9

The moral rights of Tracey Hammett and Jan McCafferty have been asserted.

Papers used by Scholastic Children's Books are made from
wood grown in sustainable forests.

To one very precious Ruby,
A huddle of heart-warming Hammetts
And a cluster of lovely friends (big and small)
Who have helped me - one and all ~ TH

With all my love to Lara Pippa who appears in this book!
Also to Kit, kisses ~ JM

Monsters Not Allowed!

Written by
Tracey Hammett

Illustrated by
Jan McCafferty

A **monster** came to
school one day.

FIDGET
SCHOOL

It tiptoed through the gate . . .

It slunk into the classroom
Grunting, **"Sorry, Monster late!"**

"What's your name?" Miss Murray asked.
It said, **"Monster forgot,"**

And while she called the register
It scratched its you-know-what.

It stomped into assembly
And did a funny walk,

While Mr Jedd the Deputy Head
Was giving a serious talk.

And then in silent reading,
While the class behaved so well,

It let out lots of silly sounds
And made a stinky smell!

It yammered, yipped and yodelled,

It warbled, whooped and whined,

Miss Murray kept it in at play,
But the monster didn't mind.

We gave it our packed lunches
And it snaffled up the lot,

It must have liked the yoghurt
'Cos it ate the spoon and pot!

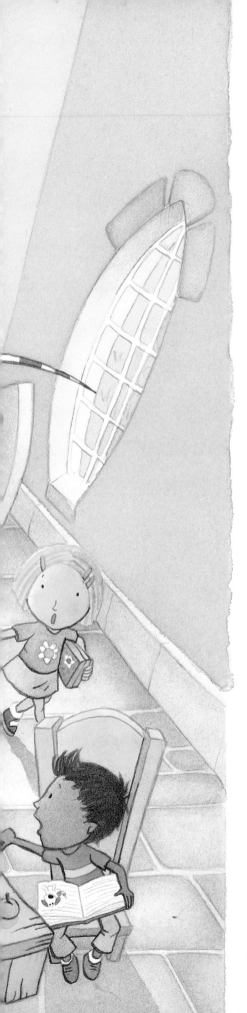

"That's not the way to eat your lunch!
Now sit up nicely, please,"
Said Mr Jedd the Deputy Head
As the monster scratched its fleas.

We had a game of football
And the monster scored a goal,

Then in PE we taught it how
To do a forward roll.

Each morning as we sat in class,
Our monster would appear,

And when we saw its funny face,
We'd all begin to cheer!

Then Mr Jedd the Deputy Head
Got very cross one day,

So he made a great big sign that said:

MONSTER,
GO
AWAY!

The monster sobbed a monster sob
And wandered down the street,

It hung its funny monster head
And dragged its monster feet.

And all at once the school went quiet –
You couldn't hear a sound.
Nobody sang, or skipped, or ran,
Or chased the leaves around.

The children wouldn't do their work,
Or play a football game,

We didn't even want our lunch –
It didn't taste the same.

"I take it back!" said Mr Jedd.
He shed a tiny tear,

"Let's find the monster right away,
And bring it straight back here!"

We all worked hard in school that day
And everyone stayed late,

We painted monster posters
And we hung them on the gate . . .

Have you seen this monster
With freckles on its nose?

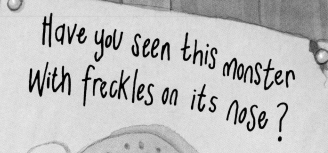

It's hairy and it's purple
from its head down to its toes.

It's a very special monster
(Although it's not polite),

FIDGET
SCHOOL

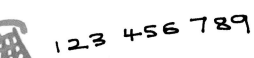

123 456 789

So if you find it, bring it back —
We promise it won't bite!

Miss Murray found the monster,
It didn't take her long . . .

She spied it in the supermarket,
Singing silly songs!

And when we brought it back to school,
It grunted, **"Monster stay!"**

So now it's joined our class for good,
And it comes in every day.

"I'm glad the monster came to school –
It's everybody's friend,"
Said Mr Jedd the Deputy Head,
Who liked it in the end.

Fidget School
END OF YEAR REPORT
Name: Monster

Mr & Mrs Monster
Googly Lane, Monsterville

Spelling:	Terrible... but top marks for trying
Maths:	Getting better every day
P.E:	Superb football skills
Music:	Fantastic yodelling
Art:	Prize for Largest Painting
Effort:	Outstanding

WELL DONE
for...

⭐ ✓ Doing all your homework

⭐ ✓ Only eating your own lunch

⭐ ✓ Not breaking any furniture

⭐ ✓ Being a wonderful friend

⭐ ✓ Just being you!

⭐ ✓ Working really hard

The End